# The PAINTER and the WILD SWANS

画家と野性の白鳥

BY CLAUDE CLÉMENT
PICTURES BY FRÉDÉRIC CLÉMENT

Dial Books for Young Readers ⌁ *New York*

First published in the United States by
Dial Books for Young Readers
A Division of NAL Penguin Inc.
2 Park Avenue, New York, New York 10016

Originally published by Duculot, Paris-Gembloux 1986
Published simultaneously in Canada by
Fitzhenry & Whiteside Limited, Toronto
Text copyright © 1986 by Claude Clément
Pictures copyright © 1986 by Frédéric Clément
Translated by Robert Levine
American text copyright © 1986 by Dial Books for Young Readers
All rights reserved
Color separation by Photolitho AG, Gossau
Printed in Belgium by Offset Printing Van den Bossche
Layout by Frédéric Clément
Typography by Sara Reynolds
COBE
3  4  5  6  7  8  9  10

Library of Congress Cataloging-in-Publication Data
Clément, Claude, 1946–   The painter and the wild swans.
Translation of: Le peintre et les cygnes sauvages.
Summary: Transfixed by the beauty of a passing flock
of white swans, a Japanese painter finds that
he cannot work until he sees them again.
[1. Fairy tales. 2. Swans—Fiction. 3. Artists—
Fiction. 4. Japan—Fiction.]
I. Clément, Frédéric, ill. II. Title.
PZ8.C5577Par 1986   [E]   86-2154
ISBN 0-8037-0268-X

*The art for each picture consists of an acrylic painting,
which is color-separated and reproduced in blue,
red, yellow, and black halftones.*

*For the photographer Teïji Saga,*
*whom I don't know, and*
*for the painter Rudo Krivos,*
*my friend.*

CLAUDE CLÉMENT

In a village in Japan there once lived a painter named Teiji who was loved by all the world. No one could equal him in capturing the beauty of the tiniest shrub, the most delicate grass, or the iris nearly in bloom. People came from far and wide to ask him to paint their portraits. So Teiji was rich and lived in great comfort.

私は思い出す　過ぎし日の事を

他人の夢をのぞくように

凍てついた羽根の上を すべる雪を

One day while he was painting out in the country, Teiji saw a flock of big white birds passing in the sky. These birds were so beautiful and sang so sweetly that he stood captivated, his eyes fixed toward the clouds, and his brush frozen in the air.

After they had passed, Teiji couldn't return to his painting. Instead he rolled up his paper, put away his brushes, and began walking toward the horizon where the birds had disappeared.

彼らに向って踏み出した

歩みの一足一足を

He walked for a long time.
In the evening he reached a fishing hut
by a large lake. There an old man greeted
him and offered him some tea. The birds
must have passed over this house, thought
Teiji. And he began asking the old man
question after question about them.
The old man just smiled.

彼らの不在を　そして静けさを

The man told Teiji how these birds came from far away, beyond the sea. Born in a frozen land called Siberia, they were wild swans. The swans lived in the snow, little spots of white on the ice fields, and when the cold grew bitter, they journeyed to a land less harsh. He said that some of them came all the way to Japan. Every year they passed over his fishing hut, singing. Then they flew over the waves before coming to rest on an island in the middle of the lake.

"Could you take me to this island
in your boat?" asked Teiji.
But the fisherman refused.
"At this time of year hunks of ice fill
the lake and it is dangerous to go out
there," he said.
So Teiji returned home.

私は思い出す

外套を脱ぐように捨てて来た生を

Soon he was among his friends again, listening to their praises of his latest paintings. But to Teiji the paintings were empty. He explained to his friends that he had caught a glimpse of real beauty and that he could not paint unless he found it again.

Then Teiji sold his house and his paintings. He kept only his brushes, his paints, and several rolls of paper. And he started back to the lake.

私は思い出す

息の青さを

水の遁意を

He made his way to the hut and begged
the fisherman to take all the money he
had in exchange for his boat.
Reluctantly the fisherman agreed.
Teiji rowed toward the middle of the
lake. He was filled with joy at the
thought of seeing the swans again.
Suddenly a gust of wind scudded a
block of ice against the hull of the frail
boat, and it capsized in the icy water.

The blood froze in Teiji's veins.
His breath all but stopped.
But he didn't want to die without
having another look at the most
beautiful thing he had seen in this
world.
Grabbing a loose board from the
wreck, he managed to reach
the shore.

私は思い出す

すべて忘れ去った事を

捜すのをやめた事を

思いもかけぬ飛翔を

He was numbed by the icy cold,
but when at last he saw the swans,
he felt warm.
They moved toward him in a soft
mist, their long necks gracefully
balanced. Teiji reached for his paints,
but when the boat had capsized his
paper and colors were soaked.
At that, sadness overcame him.
"Have I nearly died only to see
beauty slip through my hands?"
he asked himself.

その苦悩を かすか 遠くに

私は思い出す一人の男を

Then the swans gathered together.
They were preparing to fly away to
an island where the winter was milder.
When they took off and spread their
wings, the sky was darkened by a
shadow, rustling and musical.
Suddenly Teiji understood.
"It doesn't matter if an artist never
paints this. Such real beauty is rare
and impossible to capture. At least
I have seen it before I die."

そして今

鳥になり鳥にかこまれ

私は見つめている

その男の一生を

一幅の絵を見るように

As he spoke, his body was covered
by feathers and large wings
appeared at his sides.
He heard the swans, far above
the waves of the lake, and echoed
their call.
Then Teiji flew away to join his
brothers. Together they rose,
majestic and white against the
gray sky.

I remember
my former life
as a strange dream

of birds with snow gliding
from their wings

of my every step
going to greet them

of their absence
and of the silence.

I remember
leaving this life behind
the way one takes off a coat.

I remember
my icy blue breath
and the hostile, freezing water.

I remember
forgetting everything

ending the search

taking a surprise flight.

I barely remember a man,
his worries,

Today,
a bird among other birds,
I look at his life
the way one looks at a painting.

*—Teiji's poem*

画家と野性の白鳥

私は思い出す
過ぎし日の事を
他人の夢を
のぞくように
凍てついた羽根の上を
すべる雪を
彼らに向かって踏み出した
歩みの一足一足を
私は思い出す
彼らの不在を
そして静けさを
私は思い出す
外套を脱ぐように
捨てて来た生を
私は思い出す

息の青さを
水の適意を
私は思い出す
すべて忘れ去った事を
捜すのをやめた事を
思いもかけぬ飛翔を
私は思い出す
一人の男を
その苦悩を
かすか遠くに
そして今
鳥になり鳥にかこまれ
私は見つめている
その男の一生を
一幅の絵を見るように

*—Japanese translation*